The Bongles and The Crafty Crows

Written by Oscar Van Heek

Illustrated by Dean Queazy

The Bongles

Meet Big Bubba!
He's really funny.
He wears his heart on his sleeve,
and thinks with his tummy.

And this is Brainy,
with specs and all yellow.
Too clever by half,
this short little fellow.

The Twins share a tail
and look quite the same.
Double and Trouble,
by nature and name.

Meet Jessie.
She loves her clothes.
She's aways ready
to strike a pose.

This is Pet Robot.
He's made from spare parts.
He can change into anything
and is dear to their hearts.

2

3

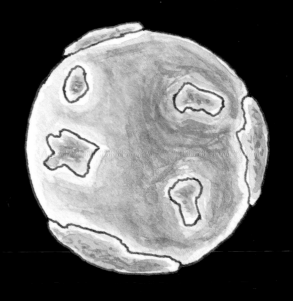

On a planet far far away,
the night was about
to make way for the day.

The Bongles were sleeping
dreaming away,
when three wooden crates
drifted in to their bay.

One full of dishes
and one full of pies
and one full of clothes,
dresses and ties.

Jessie was pleased.
She loved her new clothes,
but she'd better beware,
because so did the crows.

They dived right in
got some pants and a shoe,
flapped their wings
and off they flew.

Meanwhile Bubba was happy.
His favourite pies!
Made from fresh berries
with vegetable fries.

He took a big bite
then spotted the crows,
looking all hungry
and now wearing some clothes.

Scared they would steal
his favourite meal,
with one mighty push
he hid his crate in a bush.

The Twins meanwhile,
stared into their crate,
then grabbed some glasses,
a cup and plate.

They started juggling
and threw them up to the sky,
but the crows swooped in
and they let out a cry.

14

Now Pet had been watching
and took matters in hand.
He called everyone over,
and told them his plan.

They grabbed their crates
and away they sped,
and took their treasure
down to the shed.

But Big Bubba scoffed.
He thought he was wise.
He'd already hidden
his precious pies.

He went off to find
his hidden crate,
but soon discovered
that he was too late.

19

The crows were squawking
munching his pies,
leaping about
and eating his fries.

20

Bubba howled
and chased them away,
then joined the others,
without delay.

Now all three crates
were safely inside.
It was time for a passcode,
which Bubba supplied.

He pondered
which numbers
would padlock the door.
He puzzled some more,
then chose
one, two, three, four.

23

Now feeling happy
that no one could breach
their lock on the door,
they left for the beach.

GONE
TO
BEACH

24

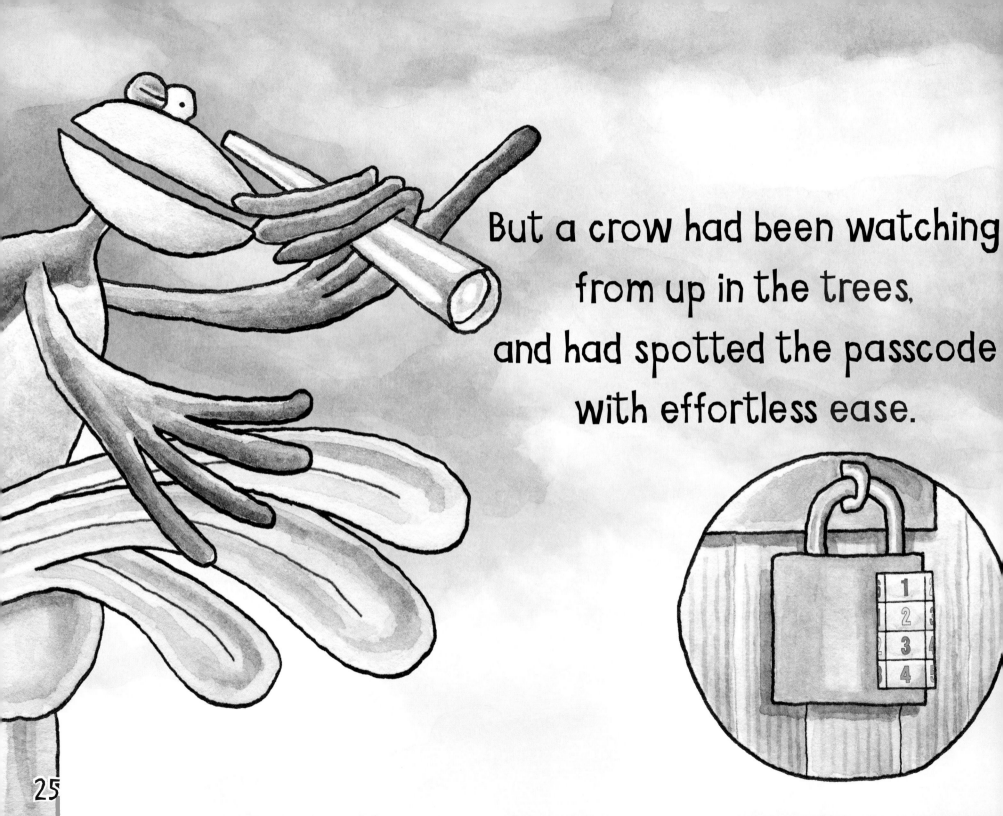

But a crow had been watching from up in the trees, and had spotted the passcode with effortless ease.

25

He swooped right down,
set the numbers all in a row,
that opened the lock.
What a clever crow!

Then another swept in
and he brought his mates,
to eat the food
and lick the plates!

Squawking about,
and munching away,
they all dressed up
and began to play.

But Pet heard their noise,
and started to shout.
Waving his arms,
he soon drove them out!

29

Pet turned his tummy
into a screen
and asked for a password
to enter in the machine.

He then asked Jessie
to stand on her toes,
and hold out her coat,
to shield them from the crows.

Bubba racked his brain,
chose three random words,
peas, trees...
and hummingbirds.

Pet extended his arms,
and reached right round the hut,
then clasped his hands tight
and locked the door shut.

Now only Bubba
could unlock the door.
For his words were the key
to keep their treasure secure.

Soon the crows flew in
and entered three words,
but guessed the wrong ones.
Those silly birds!

CUP

Now after three goes
they got such a fright,
the alarm went off,
and they all took flight!

WAAAA! WOOOOO!

36

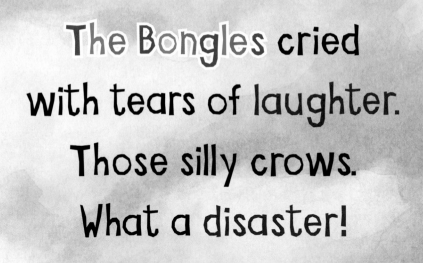

The Bongles cried
with tears of laughter.
Those silly crows.
What a disaster!

Pleased that their treasure was safe and protected, that not even the crows could steal undetected.

Jessie laid out some clothes,
they all got dressed up.
Then she gave everyone
a plate and a cup.

She set out the pies
and served up the food.
They all ate together,
and - boy - it was good!

Then Brainy filled glasses
tapped them with a twig.
He struck out a rhythm
and they all did a jig.

41

One by one,
the crows came to see.
Witnessed the dancing
and watched on in glee.

Some wearing hats,
some wearing pants,
the crows were delighted
and did their own dance.

The Bongles fell about laughing.
Those crazy crows!
Now they were friends,
and no longer foes.

Other Bongles Books

Pet Washing Machine
Monster Takeaway
Jessie and Nessie
Rubbish Island
TV Dinner

For Teachers and Parents

Visit **theBongles.com** for fun learning activities and animations.

Created and illustrated by
Dean Queazy

Written by
Oscar Van Heek

Produced by
Frances O'Neill

Graphic Design by
Viola Madau

Story by
Oscar Van Heek, Frances O'Neill, Dean Queazy

With thanks to
Calla Piercy, Luke Turner, Daniel Sellers, Louise Foreman